PENGUIN BOOKS

THE BIGGEST TONGUE IN TUNISIA AND OTHER DRAWINGS

B. Kliban's other books are *Cat, Catcalendar Cats, Never Eat Anything Bigger Than Your Head & Other Drawings, Whack Your Porcupine, Tiny Footprints, Two Guys Fooling Around with the Moon,* and *Luminous Animals and Other Drawings,* which is also available from Penguin.

The Biggest Tongue in Tunisia AND OTHER DRAWINGS

B Kliban

PENGUIN BOOKS

PENGUIN BOOKS
Viking Penguin Inc., 40 West 23rd Street,
New York, New York 10010, U.S.A.
Penguin Books Ltd, Harmondsworth,
Middlesex, England
Penguin Books Australia Ltd, Ringwood,
Victoria, Australia
Penguin Books Canada Limited, 2801 John Street,
Markham, Ontario, Canada L3R 1B4
Penguin Books (N.Z.) Ltd, 182–190 Wairau Road,
Auckland 10, New Zealand

First published in Penguin Books 1986
Published simultaneously in Canada

LIBRARY OF CONGRESS CATALOGING IN PUBLICATION DATA
Kliban, B.
The biggest tongue in Tunisia and other drawings.
1. American wit and humor, Pictorial.   I. Title.
NC1429.K58A4   1986   741.5'973   86-861
ISBN 0-14-007220-9

Printed in the United States of America by
George Banta Company Inc., Harrisonburg, Virginia

THE GOVERNMENT BURNING SURPLUS PIZZA

ALIEN TOASTER FOUND ON MOON!

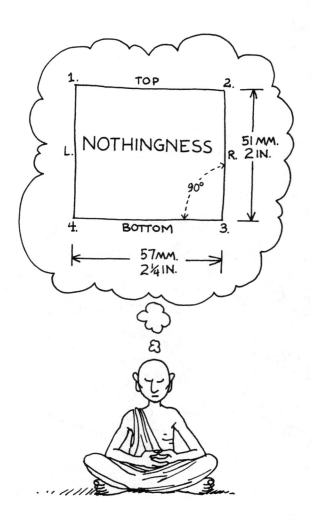

IN NEW YORK THERE IS NO SUCH THING AS A VANILLA CONE.

More Than Coincidence?

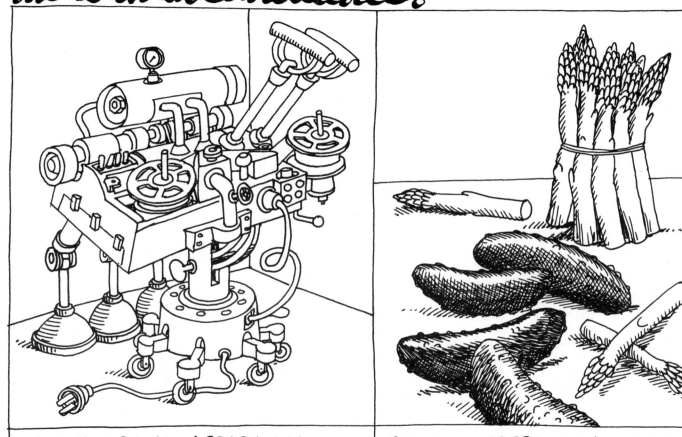

A CUMBERSOME APPARATUS

SOME CUCUMBERS AND ASPARAGUS

THE MAJOR BODILY FUNCTIONS

BENDING

JUMPING

SQUATTING

SKATING

SLICING

WIGGLING

WAITING FOR THE CAT TO DO HIS TRICK

HOWARD AND SYLVIA WERE
DEALT WITH QUICKLY AND BRUTALLY BY TIME.

THE PROTESTANT MATING RITUAL

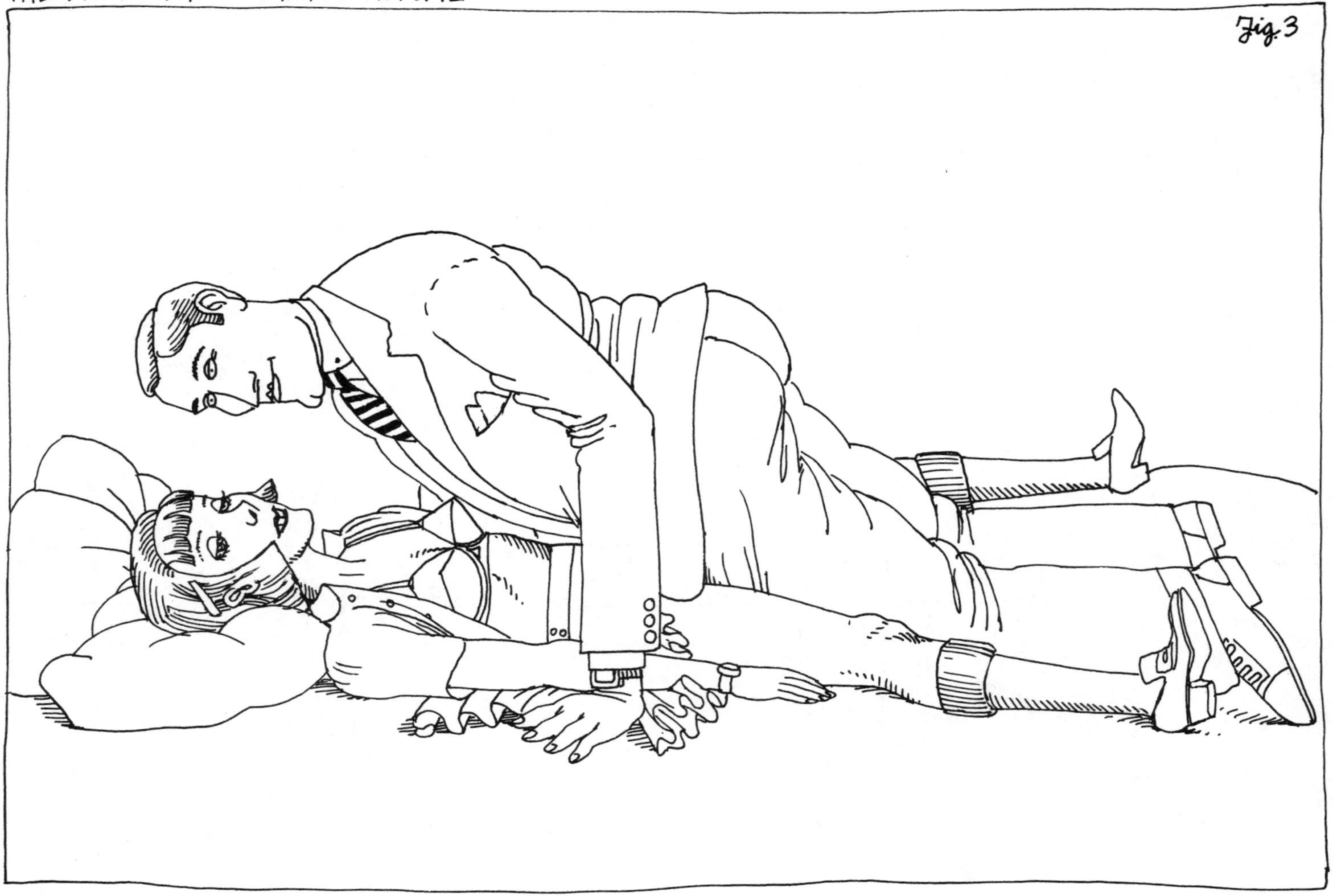

Fig. 3

The Famous Owl-in-a-Banana

OSLO, NORWAY

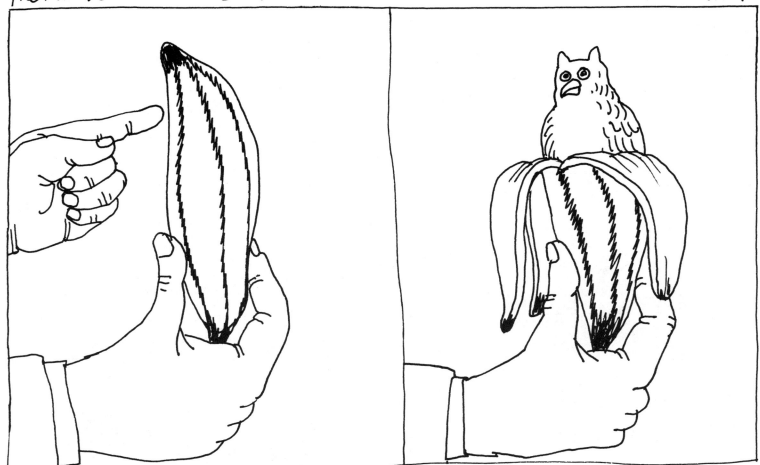

TED, FOOLING AROUND, FELL INTO A VAT OF CROUTONS AND WAS SEVERELY BREADED.

A REALLY NICE COUNTRY PLACE, WITH ANIMALS

LIFE DOWN UNDER

TURKISH VIBRATING SOUP

Espanish por Turistas

THE MARKET (EL MARKETO)

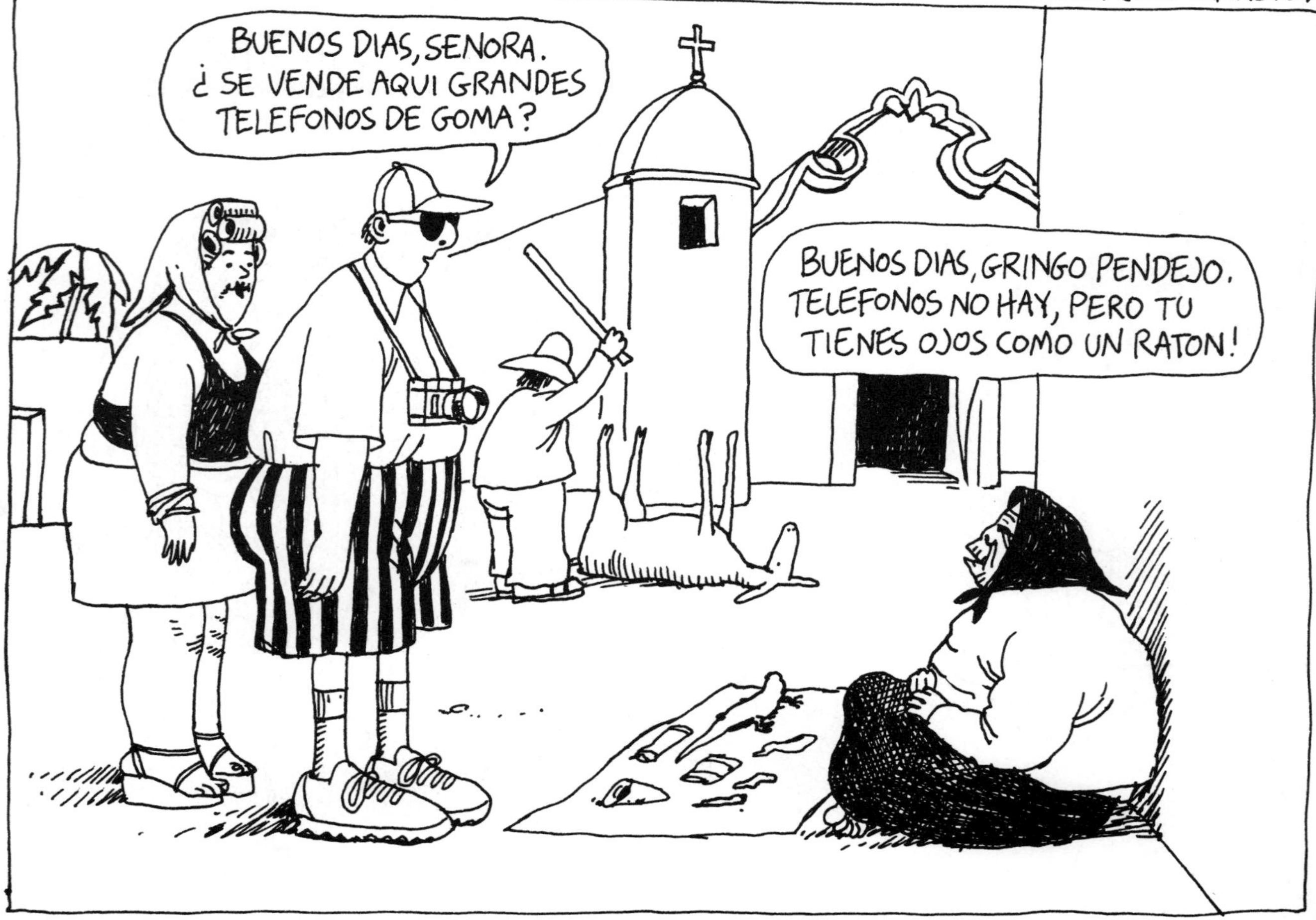

Cyclops Hats

THE EXPLORER

THE SPORTSMAN

THE ARTIST

THE WRANGLER

THE SKIPPER

THE DAREDEVIL

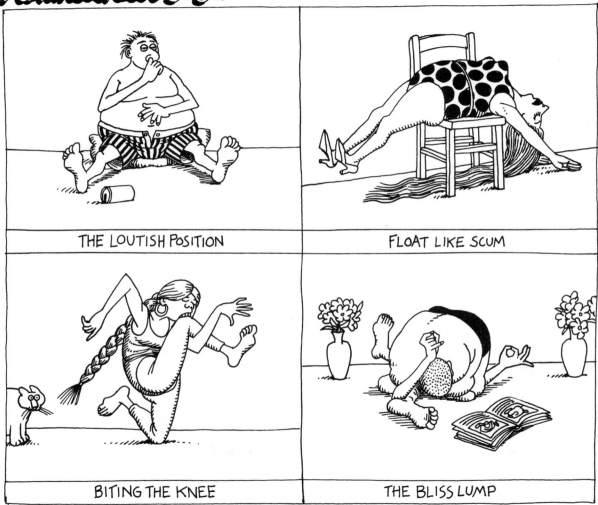

Advanced Slob Yoga

THE LOUTISH POSITION

FLOAT LIKE SCUM

BITING THE KNEE

THE BLISS LUMP

THE ROLLS RICE

The Ball We Had Last Night

A NICE DISH OF LIPS

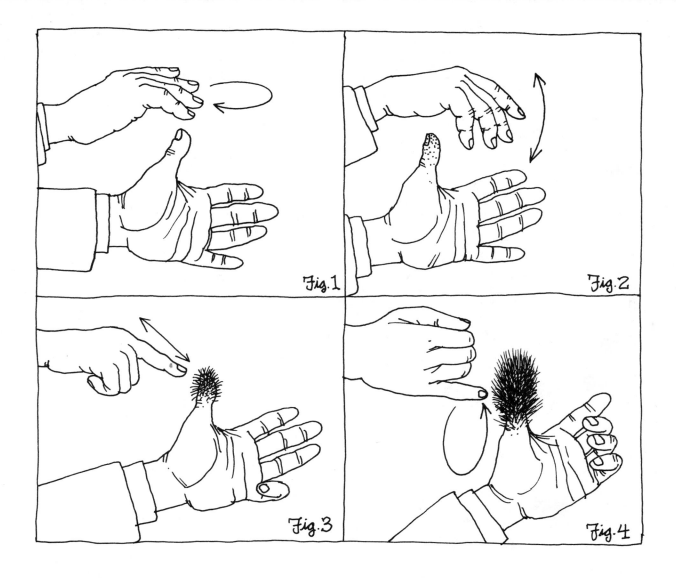

Fig.1

Fig.2

Fig.3

Fig.4

THE SENSIBLE THING TO DO WAS TO STAY IN THE VAT, WHERE IT WAS AT LEAST COOLER, BUT WESLEY, HIS JUDGEMENT DISTORTED BY THE HALLUCINOGENIC MUFFINS, DECIDED THAT HE HAD TO MAKE A BREAK FOR IT, LEAVING BEHIND NOT ONLY MADGE AND VERNON AND HIS TINY CHUM RODRIGO, THE MINIATURE POODLE, BUT ALSO THE SUPPOSEDLY IMPERVIOUS 'MIRACLE FIBER' JUMP SUIT, BOUGHT IN HOPE OF PROTECTING HIMSELF IN JUST SUCH A SITUATION, AND HIS SAMPLE CASE OF FRUIT JELLIES, DILIGENTLY CARRIED BY HAND THROUGH A VARIETY OF SIMILARLY PERILOUS IF NOT AS UNCOMFORTABLE ASSIGNMENTS, ANY ONE OF WHICH, WITH THE POSSIBLE EXCEPTION OF THIS, HE WOULD GLADLY UNDERGO AGAIN, TO PRESERVE DEMOCRACY IN CALIFORNIA.

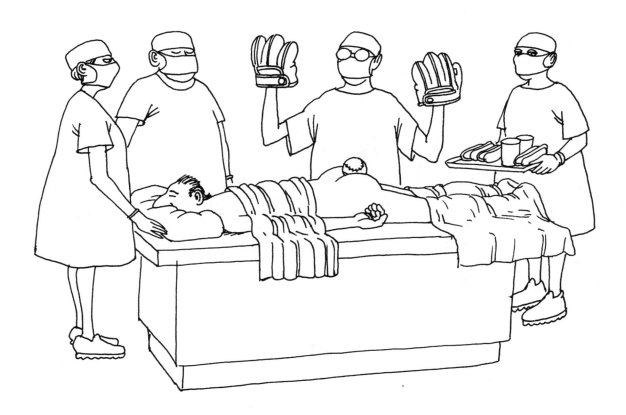

BEAR SHITS NECKTIES!

The Papal Court

LIGHT TRAVELS AT 186,000 MILES A SECOND.

ANY FASTER WOULD BE DANGEROUS.

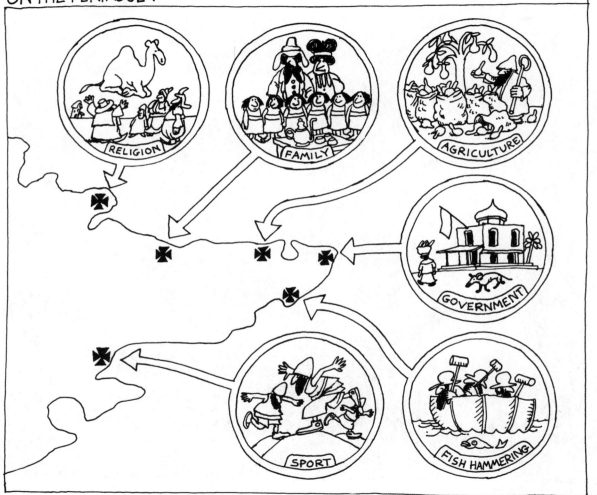

RUNK POCKERS
POCK RUNKERS

SENSIBLE SHOES

A Little Family History

WHEN I WENT TO ART SCHOOL, WE DIDN'T
HAVE IT EASY, LIKE KIDS DO NOWDAYS!

AN IDEA DESTROYING ITSELF BY PERCEPTION

AN ANGEL OF THE LORD SMITES A CARELESS JAYWALKER

CLOUDS TURNING INTO IRON AND FALLING ON EVERYTHING

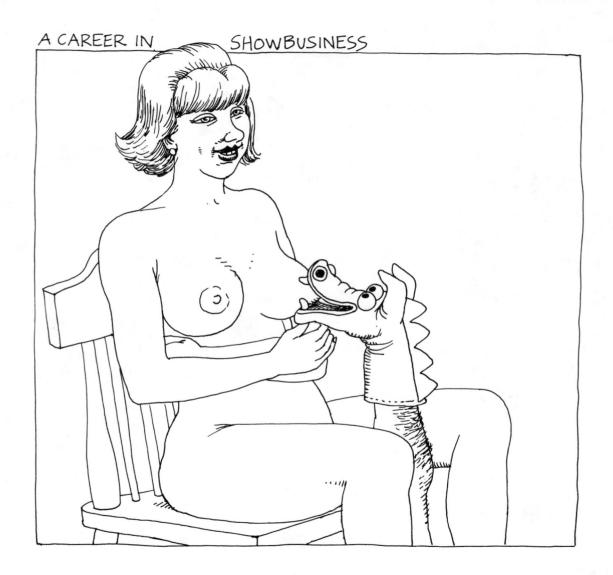

A Little Family History

THE IROQUOIS CORN HARMONICA

KILL THE SONOFABITCH! KNOCK HIS FUCKIN HEAD OFF!

PORTUGAL

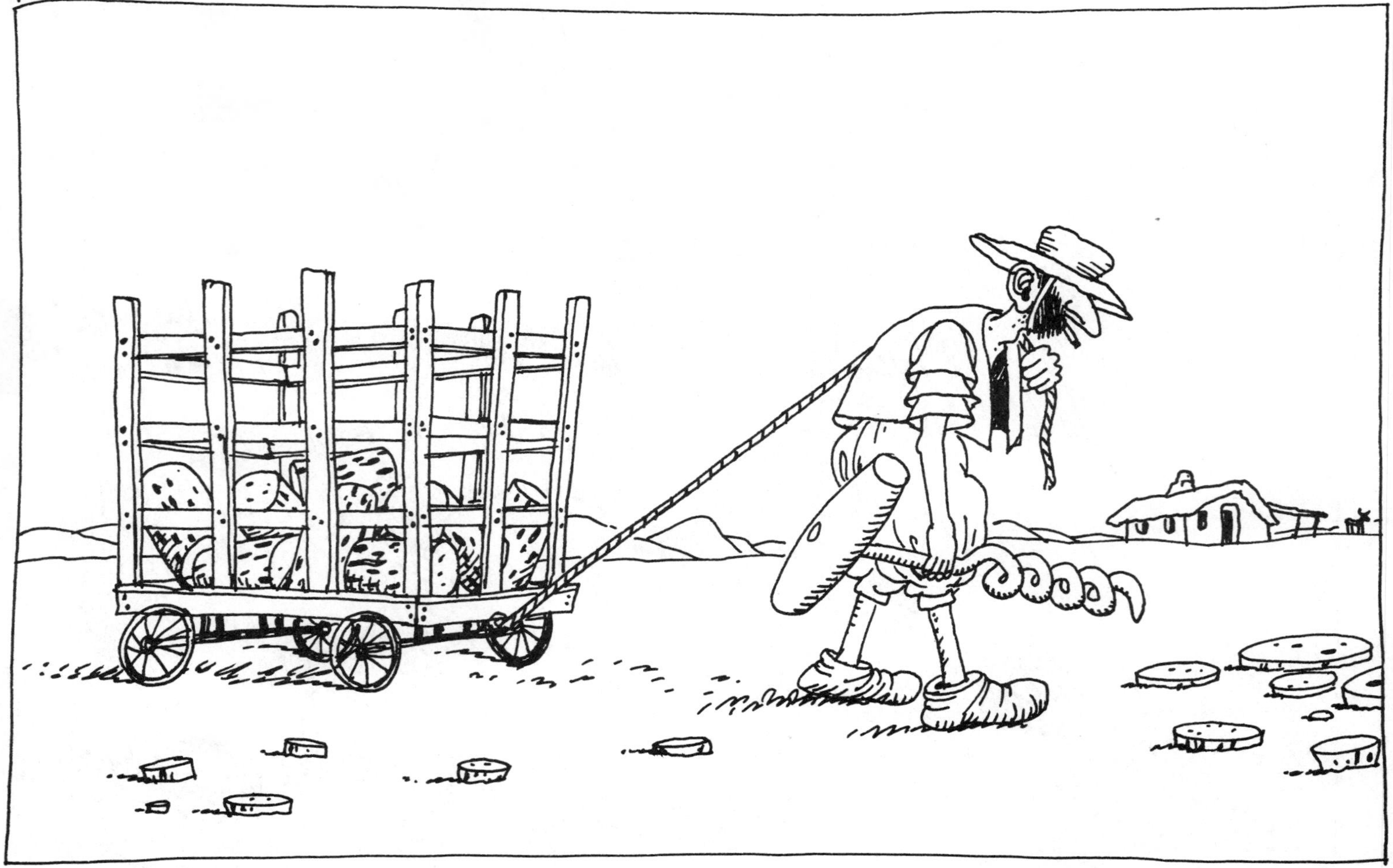

Inglese

Fig. 1 — MAN EATING SHARK

Fig. 2 — MAN EATING HAMBURGERS

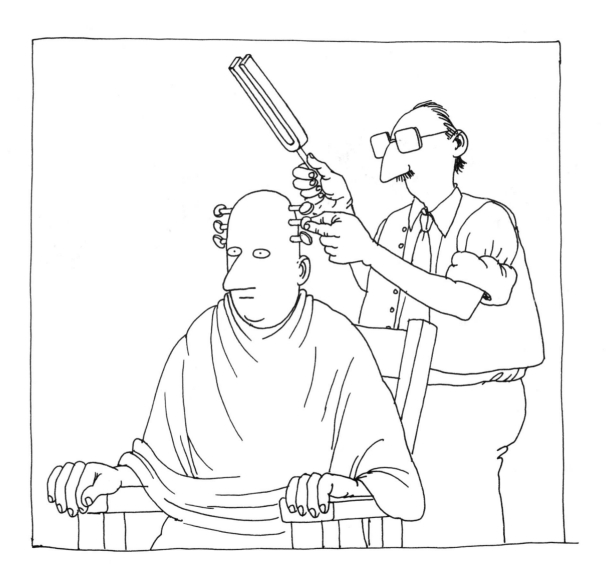

SALLY, THE HOME ENTERTAINMENT CENTER

AND THE LORD SMOTE THE BABYLONIANS WITH MODEL TRAINS, AND GRIEVED THEM SORELY.

EATERS OF DUNG

RESEMBLANCE POWDER

THE HEAD COLD

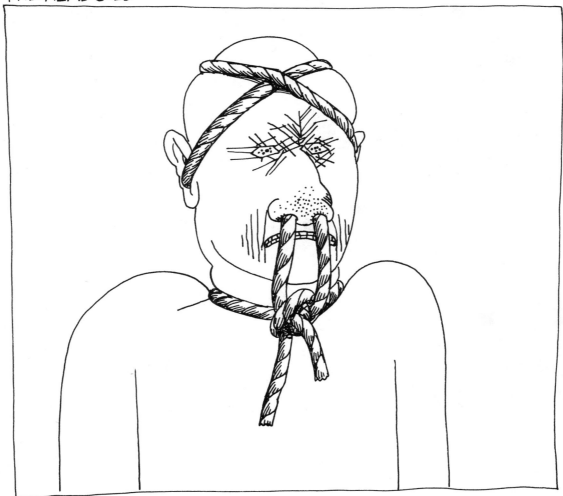

BROUGHT DOWN ON THE FORTY YARD LINE BY ESTHER WILLIAMS

GOD GAVE US THESE BODIES BECAUSE HE HAS BETTER ONES AT HOME.

THERE ONCE LIVED IN THE VILLAGE OF R., A CERTAIN WALDEMAR, A CARVER OF LETTUCE, RENOWNED FOR HIS LIKENESSES OF THE KING, A HALFWIT.

THE FUNDAMENTAL FAMILY

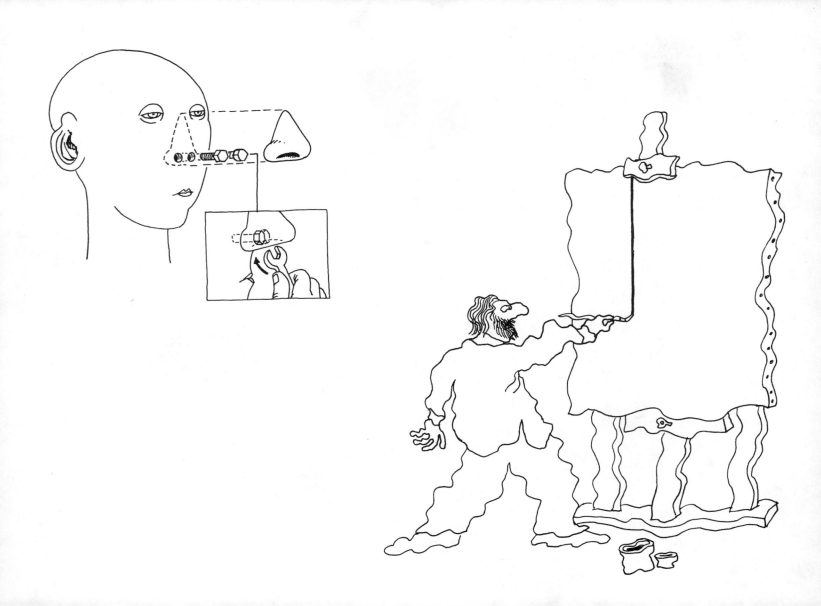

MY SON, I HAVE SEEN MANY THINGS IN SIXTY YEARS BY THIS RIVER, BUT NEVER A STUFFED PANDA.

THE MARIJUANA PLANT

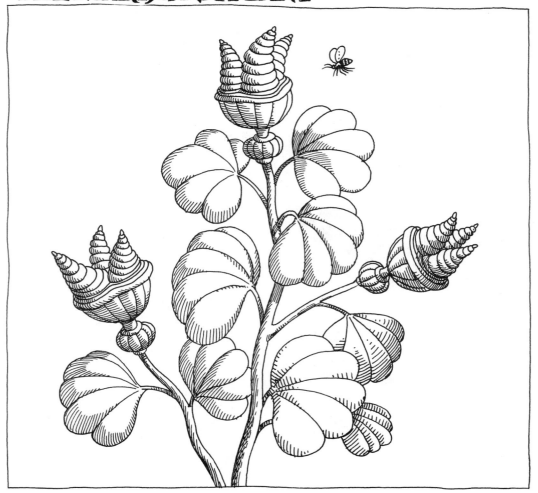

JEWISH MUSIC

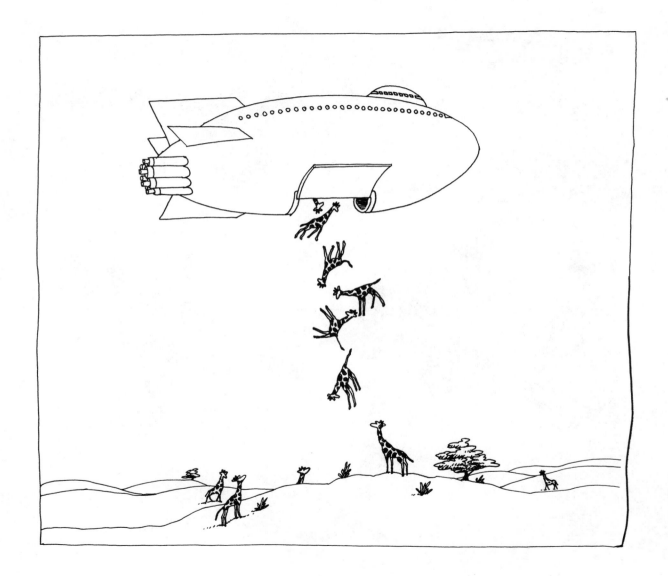

ONE BRIGHT SUNNY SUNDAY MORNING, LITTLE FLORENCE THE HOT DOG PUT ON HER MOST COMFORTABLE BUN, BECAUSE TODAY WAS PICNIC DAY, AND THE WHOLE FAMILY WAS INCLUDED ◇ OFF THROUGH THE WOODS AND FIELDS THEY WENT... FATHER, MOTHER, MONROE, LUCILLE AND THE TWINS HAROLD AND HAROLDINE, FROLICKING AND LEAPING THROUGH THE GRASS AND FERNS ◇

FLORENCE, WHO HAD BEEN LAGGING BEHIND AND NOT PAYING ATTENTION, HURRIED TO CATCH UP AND TRIPPED, TUMBLING END OVER END DOWN A GULLY, HER BUN CRUELLY TORN AWAY BY THORNS AND BRANCHES ◇ DAZED, SHE STOOD UP AND REALIZED THAT SHE WAS NOT ONLY BUNLESS, BUT LOST AS WELL ◇ STRUGGLING BACK UP THE HILL, SHE PICKED A DIRECTION SHE HOPED THE FAMILY HAD GONE IN, AND HEADED INTO THE WOODS TO FIND THEM

AFTER AN HOUR OR SO OF SEARCHING, FLORENCE WAS TOTALLY LOST, AND TRYING NOT TO PANIC, SHE SLUMPED AGAINST A ROCK TO COLLECT HERSELF AND THINK ABOUT WHAT TO DO NEXT ◇ LISTENING VAGUELY TO THE FOREST SOUNDS, SHE BECAME AWARE OF VOICES, SPEAKING A LANGUAGE SHE DIDN'T UNDERSTAND ◇ HUNCHING LOW IN THE GRASS, SHE CAUTIOUSLY MADE HER WAY TOWARD THEM ◇ FROM BEHIND A LOG, SHE SLOWLY RAISED HERSELF AND PEEKED OVER ◇ WHAT SHE SAW MADE HER STUFFING BOIL ◇ IT WAS A STRATEGICALLY PLACED NAZI MACHINE GUN NEST, WITH THREE MACHINE GUNNERS ARMED TO THE TEETH, BUT NOTHING IS AS AMERICAN AS A HOT DOG, AND WITHOUT A THOUGHT FOR HER SAFETY, FLORENCE LEAPT FROM HER HIDING PLACE AND ATTACKED, SQUIRTING DEADLY HOT DOG JUICES ALL OVER THE NAZIS, WHO WERE TAKEN TOTALLY BY SURPRISE AND SOON RENDERED SENSELESS.

DAYS LATER, AN EXHAUSTED FLORENCE WAS FOUND BY A GROUP OF YOUNG KNOCKWURSTS OUT ON A HIKE, AND BROUGHT HOME TO HER GRATEFUL FAMILY AND THE MEDIA PEOPLE, WHO MADE HER A NATIONAL HERO ◇ SHE WAS EVENTUALLY AWARDED THE CONGRESSIONAL MEDAL OF HONOR BY THE PRESIDENT HIMSELF ◇ LATER THAT DAY THE PRESIDENT'S DOG ATE HER BY MISTAKE, BUT SHE IS FONDLY REMEMBERED BY HER FAMILY AND MANY FRIENDS. ◇

JIU JITSU

CHRISTIAN JITSU

THE PLAINS OF AMERICA, COVERED BY VAST HERDS OF LAWYERS

THE FOOD AND DRUG ADMINISTRATION

THE BOOKBURNING FESTIVAL WAS CALLED OFF BECAUSE NOBODY HAD ANY.

the Drawing Machine

AT FIRST IT WAS VERY LARGE AND COULD ONLY DRAW WIGGLY LINES, BUT AFTER A FEW IMPROVEMENTS AND ADJUSTMENTS, THE INVENTOR HAD IT TURNING OUT MECHANICAL DRAWINGS OF FAIR QUALITY.

LATER, WHEN IT WAS ELECTRIFIED AND VASTLY IMPROVED, IT WOULD DRAW JUST ABOUT ANYTHING HE WANTED IT TO, BUT WAS DIFFICULT TO OPERATE, AND SUBJECT TO FREQUENT BREAKDOWNS OF ITS MANY TINY LEVERS AND PULLEYS.

EVENTUALLY THESE PROBLEMS WERE CORRECTED, AND WITH THE ADVENT OF ELECTRONICS, THE INVENTOR INSTALLED A VOICE COMMAND DEVICE, SO ALL HE HAD TO DO WAS PUT IN A ROLL OF PAPER, SIT BACK IN A COMFORTABLE CHAIR AND TELL IT WHAT TO DRAW, OR EVEN PUT IT ON "AUTO" AND LET IT DRAW ALL BY ITSELF.

HE HAD THE MACHINE DRAWING SOME REALLY STRANGE THINGS, TO THE POINT WHERE IT WOULD HEAT UP DANGEROUSLY, BUT HE GOT TIRED OF FOOLING AROUND WITH IT ANYHOW, AND PUT IT IN HIS GARAGE WHERE I FOUND IT ABOUT TWENTY-FIVE YEARS AGO.

IT WRITES A LITTLE, TOO.